JELLYBEANS FOR GIANTS

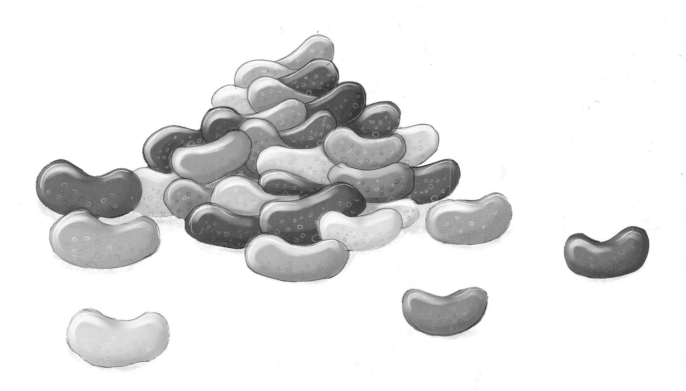

Adam & Charlotte Guillain • Lee Wildish

EGMONT

A boy called George had a breathtaking thought,
That giants might really exist.
"We just need a beanstalk," George said to his dog,
"And a gift that a giant can't resist."

So George poured some jellybeans into his bag,

But he kept one to plant in a pot.

He watered the bean and the very next day . . .

...a **beanstalk** had grown - quite a lot!

"It's **ginormous!**" George cheered.

"Come on, Trixie, let's go!"

He heaved up his bag filled with treats.

"The giant is bound to be friendly," said George.

"Even big people love to get sweets."

As Trixie and George clambered higher and higher,
They heard a voice sing, loud and strong.
"Could **that** be a giant?" George said to his dog . . .

But a pixie was singing the song!

"If you're looking for giants," the pixie told George,

"You'll need to keep climbing up high."

Then she plucked something fluffy and pink from a branch,

And she grinned, "But it's quicker to fly!"

George took a small bite, then cried,

"Candyfloss - yum!

Here, Trixie, there's plenty to share."

They guzzled up more until, to their surprise . . .

. . . they floated up into the air!

"We're flying!" whooped George, as they rose up and up.

"Now we'll track down a giant in a flash."

But, all of a sudden, the magic ran out,
And they fell with a "Whoops!" and a . . .

CRASH!

"Ouch!" George complained, and he peered all around.

There were huge purple fruits everywhere.

"These have to belong to a giant," said George.

Then a horrible smell filled the air.

"Yuck!" grimaced George, holding on to his nose,
"A giant smells worse than you'd think."

The whole beanstalk shook as loud footsteps approached . . .

"It's a troll!" exclaimed George.

"What a stink!"

When the troll spotted George, he held up a large spoon,

And waved it towards a huge pot!

"Oh, Trixie! He wants us for lunch," stammered George . . .

"Oh, no!" boomed the troll. "I do **not!**"

"I'm harvesting grumpkins," he said with a grin,
"To put in my fine grumpkin stew.

You must come and taste it - my cooking is great!"
And he held out a ladle of goo.

George sniffed the troll's stew and
  he pulled a grim face,
The steaming hot gunk made him wheeze.
The troll put a sprinkle of pepper on top,
Then let out . . .

. . . a whopping big **sneeze!**

They shot up the beanstalk, propelled by the blast,

And were covered in gunge, thick and green.

They came down to land with
an almighty **bounce**
On what seemed like . . .

. . . a **huge** trampoline!

"This **has** to belong to a giant!" cheered George.
"At last we are having some luck!"

But he looked down and saw that his feet couldn't move
And that he and his dog were now stuck!

"This isn't a trampoline, Trixie," said George,
"And what is that scuttling sound?"
Then eight gangly legs tiptoed on to the web,
As Trixie and George spun around . . .

"A huge hairy **spider**!" George stammered, "Oh, no!
Are you going to eat us for tea?"

"Of course not!" the spider laughed, scurrying up.
"I'll soon set the two of you free."

But just as the spider was cutting them loose,
The massive web started to sway.
A loud, booming voice called out,
"FEE-FI-FO-FUM!"

George gaped at the hand
that was holding them up,
And two huge bright eyes
twinkled back.
"A giant!" George shouted.
"I've found you at last!"
But the giant said,
"I need a snack!"

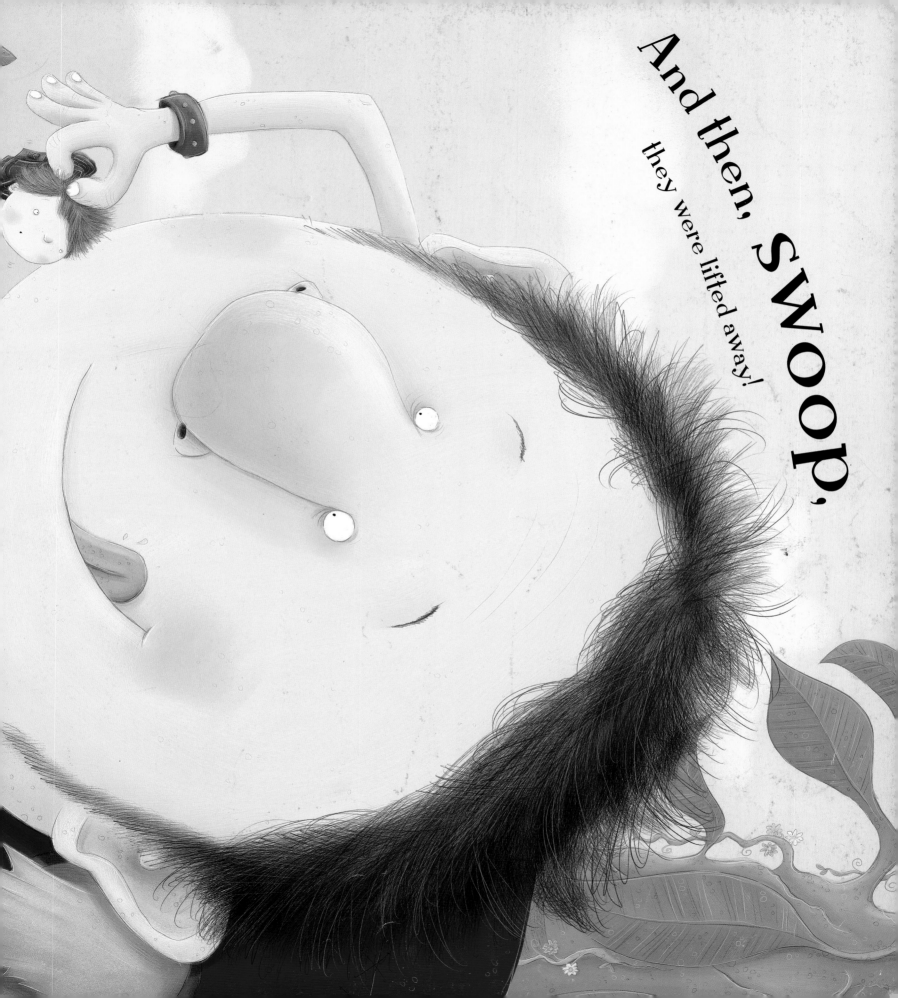

And then, **SWOOP**, they were lifted away!

"Don't eat us!" cried George, and he reached for his bag.
"I've brought you some jellybeans – here!"

But his backpack was empty. "Oh, no! They've all gone!"
Trixie started to tremble with fear.

But just as George thought he'd be gobbled right up,
A sight made his eyes open wide.

"What's in those green pods?" he called out to the giant.
"Could there be something tasty inside?"

George picked a large pod and he gave it a squeeze –
Then he gasped at the rainbow within.
Bright jellybeans tumbled out.
"Yum!" said the giant.

"My favourites!" he roared with a grin.

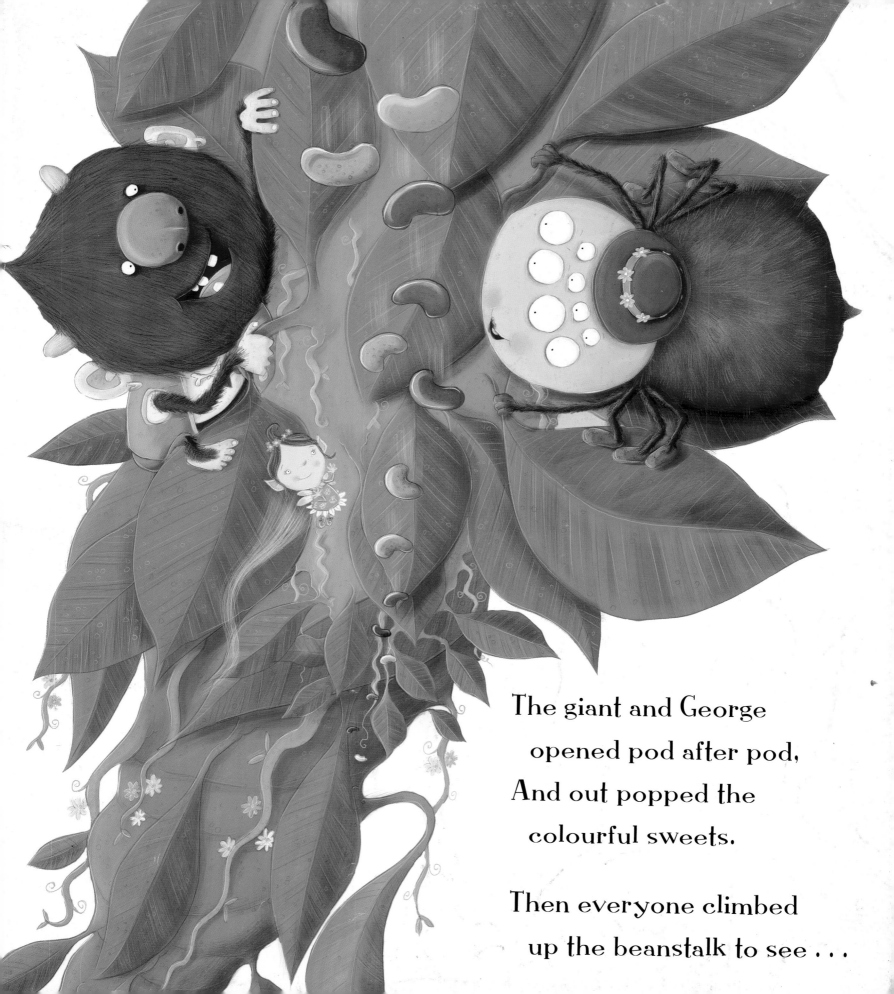

The giant and George
opened pod after pod,
And out popped the
colourful sweets.

Then everyone climbed
up the beanstalk to see . . .

And they feasted on **jellybean treats!**

To Louis, Oliver and Frey xx

A&C Guillain

EGMONT
We bring stories to life

First published in Great Britain 2018 by Egmont UK Limited
The Yellow Building, 1 Nicholas Road, London W11 4AN

www.egmont.co.uk

Text copyright © Adam and Charlotte Guillain 2018
Illustrations copyright © Lee Wildish 2018

The moral rights of the authors and illustrator have been asserted.

ISBN 978 1 4052 8524 7 (Paperback)

A CIP catalogue record for this title is available from the British Library.